Ziggy
Learns his ABC's

by Corinne Schmid
Illustrated by Andreea Togoe

First Printing, 2018
ISBN (paperback): 978-0-9947306-3-3
ISBN (eBook): 978-0-9947306-4-0
ISBN (hardcover): 979-0-9947306-6-4

Other Titles
Ziggy Catches a Cold (2018)

www.ZiggytheIggy.com

For Olivia and Lucas

Ziggy the Iggy is a little pup,
with much to learn as he grows up.
His sister Twiggy teaches him his ABCs.
Using fun words, learning is a breeze!

And so little Ziggy will not forget,
this book has all the letters of the alphabet.

A a airplane

Ziggy flies on an airplane when he and Twiggy go on vacation.

bone b B

Ziggy enjoys eating a dog bone. It is his favorite treat!

C c  collar

Ziggy wears a blue dog collar. His sister Twiggy wears a pink collar.

dance

Ziggy and Twiggy
love dancing to their
favorite Iggy music.

E e ears

Twiggy points
her ears to
show that it was
Ziggy!

fur  **f F**

Ziggy does not need a haircut because his fur is very short.

G g greyhound

Ziggy plays with his bigger greyhound friend at the dog park.

house

This is the house where
Ziggy and Twiggy live.

Ii Italy

Twiggy teaches her brother Ziggy all about the country, Italy.

jump j J

Ziggy likes to
jump for joy when
he plays outside.

K k kiss

Ziggy gives
his sister Twiggy
a big Iggy kiss.

leash

Ziggy needs his leash
to go for a walk.

M m mail

Ziggy fetches the mail
from the mailbox.

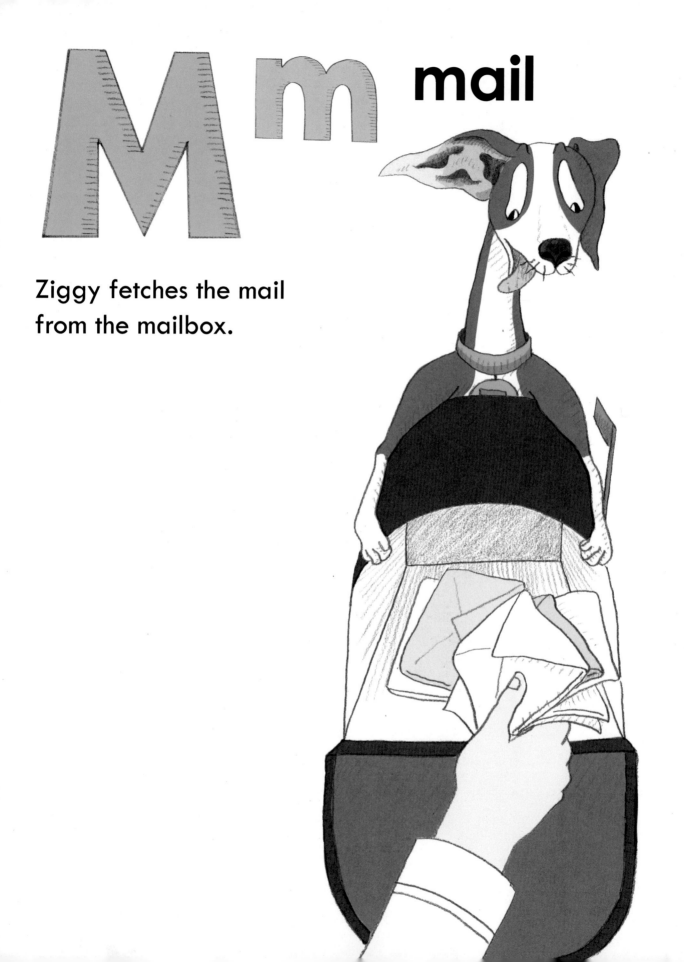

nap

Ziggy takes an afternoon nap every day.

outside

Ziggy likes to play outside on warm, sunny days.

paws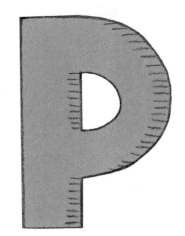

Ziggy needs four
shoes to cover his
four Iggy paws.

Q q quilt

Twiggy made this quilt for Ziggy. It is his favorite blanket.

run

Ziggy can run very fast.

S s sweater

Ziggy wears a warm sweater on cold days.

tail

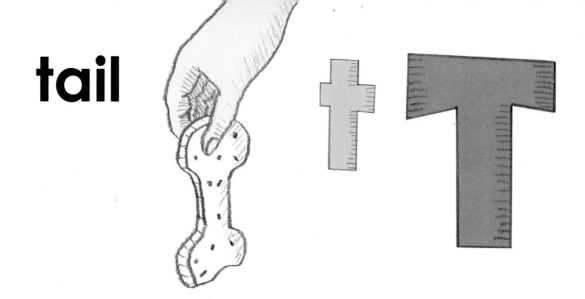

t T

Ziggy wags his tail
when he gets a treat.

U u umbrella

Ziggy uses an umbrella to stay dry when it rains.

vacuum V V

Ziggy helps vacuum the floor.

W w walk

The only thing Ziggy
loves more than
a walk,
is two!

xylophone Xx

Ziggy plays the xylophone for Twiggy.

Y y yawn

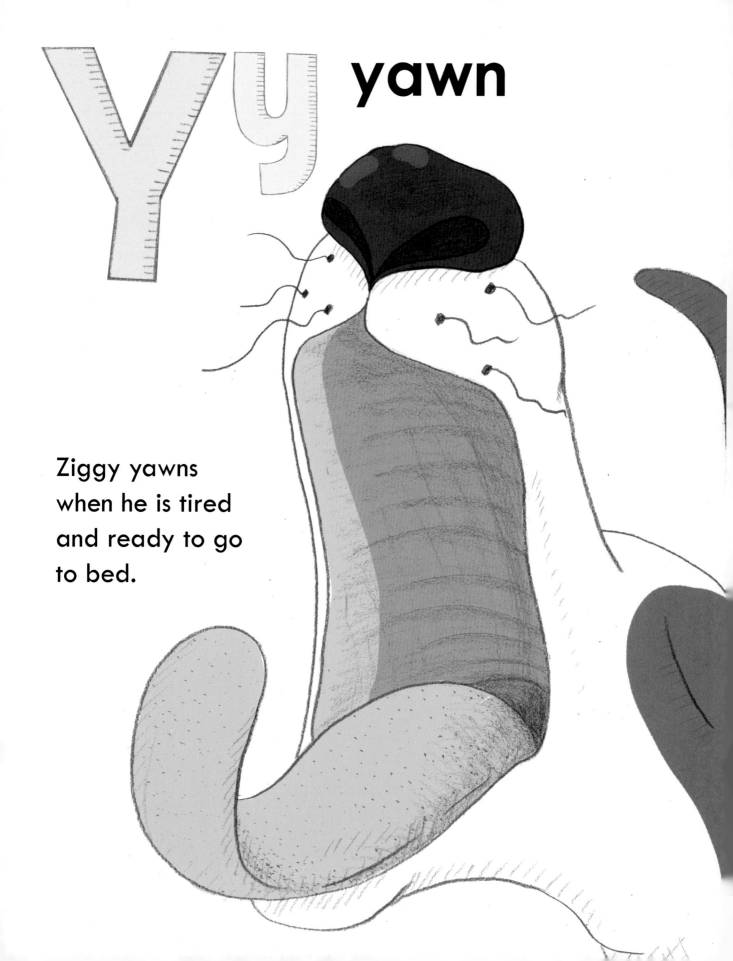

Ziggy yawns when he is tired and ready to go to bed.

Ziggy

Ziggy is a cute
little Iggy.

84750701R00020

Made in the USA
San Bernardino, CA
11 August 2018